Two Viking Romances

P9-BZI-099

PENGUIN BOOKS

PENGUIN BOOKS

Published by the Penguin Group

Penguin Books USA Inc., 375 Hudson Street,
New York, New York 10014, U.S.A.
Penguin Books Ltd, 27 Wrights Lane,
London W8 5TZ, England
Penguin Books Australia Ltd, Ringwood,
Victoria, Australia
Penguin Books Canada Ltd, 10 Alcorn Avenue,
Toronto, Ontario, Canada M4V 3B2
Penguin Books (N.Z.) Ltd, 182–190 Wairau Road,
Auckland 10, New Zealand

Penguin Books Ltd, Registered Offices:
Harmondsworth, Middlesex, England

Published in Penguin Books 1995

Translation copyright © Hermann Pálsson and Paul Edwards, 1985
All rights reserved

These stories are from *Seven Viking Romances*,
translated by Hermann Pálsson and Paul Edwards,
published by Penguin Books.

ISBN 0 14 60.0156 7

Printed in the United States of America

Two Viking Romances

CONTENTS

Bosi and Herraud

There was a king called Hring who ruled over East Gotaland. His father was King Gauti, the son of King Odin of Sweden. Odin had travelled all the way from Asia, and all the noblest royal families in Scandinavia are descended from him. Hring's half-brother on his father's side was Gautrek the Generous, but his mother's family was just as distinguished.

Hring was married to a fine-looking, even-tempered woman called Sylgja, the daughter of Earl Seafarer of the Smalands. She had two brothers called Dayfarer and Nightfarer, both retainers of King Harald Wartooth, who at that time ruled over Denmark and the greater part of Scandinavia besides.

Hring and his queen had a son called Herraud. He was a tall handsome man, strong and talented, a man with very few equals. Everyone was very fond of Herraud, except his own father who had no great liking for him. As it happened, the king had another son, who was illegitimate, and he was fonder of him than he was of Herraud. This bastard son was called Purse and at this time he was a grown man, as the king had begotten him when he was still young. The king granted Purse large estates and made him his counsellor and tax collector. Purse was in charge of levies and fee-estates, and he controlled the king's revenues and expenses. Most people found him very grasping in collecting the money and equally tight-fisted when he had to pay it out. But he was loyal to the king and always had his interests at heart, and so his name became a household word and people are called Pursers who look after your interests and guard them with care.

To store the silver that was paid as dues to the king, Purse used certain money bags which have been known as purses ever since. But what he collected over and above the rightful amount he used to set aside in smaller money bags which he called profit-purses. He used this money for expenses, leaving the main tribute intact. Purse was not a particularly popular man, but the king was very fond of him and let him have his own way in everything.

BOSI'S FAMILY

There was a man called Thvari or Bryn-Thvari, who lived not far from the king's residence. He had been a great viking in his younger years and during his fighting career he had come up against an amazon, Brynhild, the daughter of King Agnar of Noatown. They had set about one another, and soon Brynhild was wounded and unable to carry on fighting. Then Thvari took her into his care, along with a great deal of money. He saw to it that her wounds were fully healed, but she remained bent and twisted for the rest of her life, and so she was known as

Stunt-Brynhild. Thvari made her his wife, and although she wore a helmet and coat of mail at her wedding, their married life was a happy one.

After that Thvari retired from viking life and settled down on a farm. He and Brynhild had two sons. The elder, Smid, was not very big, but exceptionally good-looking, highly talented and extremely clever with his hands. The younger son, Bosi, was a tall strong fellow, swarthy and not so handsome. A cheerful, humorous man, he took after his mother in personality and looks. Whatever he started, he would see it through, and he never flinched, no matter whom he had to deal with. His mother was very fond of him, and so he was nicknamed after her and called Stunt-Bosi. He was a great joker both in what he said and did, so the name suited him well.

There was an old woman called Busla, who had been Thvari's concubine, and fostered his sons for him. Busla was highly skilled in magic. She found Smid more amenable than his brother and taught him a great deal. She offered to tutor Bosi in magic as well, but he said he didn't want it written in his saga that he'd carried anything through by trickery instead of relying on his own manhood.

The king's son Herraud and the brothers were much of an age, and they were also close friends. Bosi spent a lot of time at the royal court, where he and Herraud were always together. Purse often complained that Herraud used to give clothes to Bosi, since Bosi's clothes were always getting torn. Bosi was considered a bit rough when he was playing with the other boys, but no one dared complain about it because of Herraud who always took his side. In the end, Purse asked the king's men to give Bosi such a rough time that he'd stop playing.

BOSI JOINS HERRAUD'S EXPEDITION

On one occasion when the ball-game was getting a bit out of hand, the king's men started pushing Bosi around but he hit back and one of them dislocated an arm. The next day he broke someone's leg. On the third day two men went for him and a number of others got in his way. He knocked out the eye of one of them with the ball, and threw the other to the ground, breaking his neck. The king's men rushed for their weapons with the idea of killing Bosi, but Herraud stood by him with all the men he could get. They came very close to fighting, until the king turned up. At Purse's insistence the king made Bosi an outlaw, but Herraud helped him to escape so he wasn't caught.

A little later Herraud asked his father to give him some warships and sturdy men as he wanted to sail away and, if possible, earn himself a reputation. The king put the matter to Purse, who answered that in his opinion the treasury would soon be empty if Herraud was to get all the outfit he wanted. The king said they would have to grant the request, and he got his own way. So preparations were made for Herraud's expedition and no cost was spared, for he was very particular about everything. He and Purse didn't see eye to eye over this.

Herraud set off with five ships, most of them old. He had brave men with him and a great deal of money, both gold and silver, and with this he sailed away from Gotaland south to Denmark.

One stormy day they saw a man standing on a cliff. He called out, asking them for a passage, but Herraud said he wasn't going out of his way for him, though he was welcome provided he could catch the ship. The man jumped off the cliff and landed on the tiller that jutted out from the helm, a leap of fifteen yards. Then everyone realized that it was Bosi. Herraud was delighted to see him and asked him to be the forecastleman on his own ship. From there they sailed to Saxony, plundering wherever they went, and getting plenty of money.

So it went on for five years.

BOSI KILLS PURSE

Meanwhile, back in Gotaland, after Herraud had gone away, Purse inspected his father's treasury. When he saw that the coffers and bags were empty, he said the same thing over and over again. 'I remember the days,' he said, 'when this treasury was a happier sight.'

Then Purse set off to collect the royal tributes and taxes and was very exacting in most of his demands. He came to Thvari and ordered him to pay his levies as others did, but Thvari answered that he was old enough to be exempt from the levy and refused to pay. Purse said that Thvari's responsibility was even greater than other men's, since it was his fault that Herraud had left the country. He also wanted compensation for the men Bosi had injured, but Thvari said that anyone who played in a game had to look out for himself, and that he wasn't going to throw away his money on that account. This led to a heated argument between them and eventually Purse forced his way into Thvari's store-room and took away two chests full of gold and plenty of other valuables, including weapons and clothes. After that they parted. Purse went back home with a great deal of money and told the king what had happened. The king told him it had been a mistake to rob Thvari as he would later find out to his cost, but Purse said that he wasn't in the least concerned.

Meanwhile, as Herraud and Bosi were getting ready to sail back home from their expedition, they heard about how Purse had robbed Thvari. Herraud decided then to try to set things right for Bosi and bring about a reconciliation between him and the king. They ran into a gale so fierce that their ships were driven apart, and all the ships that Herraud had brought from home were lost, but with two other ships he managed to reach Elfar Skerries.

Bosi's ship was driven to Wendland. Shortly before, Purse had also arrived there with two ships from the Baltic countries where he'd bought some fine treasures for the king. When Bosi realized this, he told his men to arm themselves, then went to see Purse and asked him when he was going to pay back what he'd stolen from Thvari. Purse replied that Bosi was making a pretty impudent suggestion, since he'd already been outlawed by the king, and ought to count himself lucky if he lost no more than this. Then both sides seized their weapons and started fighting. The outcome was that Bosi killed Purse, and then spared the lives of all the rest, but he seized the ships and all that was on board.

As soon as he got a favourable wind, Bosi sailed over to Gotaland, where he found his foster-brother Herraud and told him what had happened. Herraud said that this wouldn't exactly endear him to the king. 'Why come to me when you've dealt me such a near blow?' he said.

'I knew that I'd never be able to escape you if you wanted revenge,' said Bosi, 'and anyway, you seemed to be the only person I could turn to.'

'It's true enough,' said Herraud, 'that Purse was no great loss, even though he was my kinsman. I'm going to see my father and try to reconcile you.'

Bosi said he didn't expect any great treatment from the king, but Herraud said they ought to try everything they could. So he went to see his father, and greeted him respectfully. His father received him coldly, as he'd already been told what had happened between Bosi and Purse.

Herraud said to his father, 'You've every right to demand compensation from my friend Bosi, he's made a great deal of mischief. He's killed your son Purse, though it wasn't without provocation. We'd like to make a settlement and offer you as much money as you wish. In addition, we'll agree to pledge our loyal support and Bosi is willing to serve you in any way you like.'

The king replied angrily, 'Herraud, you're very determined to help this ruffian, but plenty of people would have thought it more your duty to avenge your brother and our disgrace.'

'Purse was no great loss,' said Herraud. 'I'm not even certain whether or not he was my brother, even though you were so fond of him. It seems to me you're showing me very little respect when you refuse to accept a reconciliation in spite of the plea I've made, and in my opinion, I'm offering a better man than Purse to take his place.'

The king had grown very angry and said, 'Your pleading on Bosi's behalf can only make matters worse. As soon as he's caught he'll be hanged on a gallows higher than any thief has ever been hanged before.'

Herraud was angry too. 'There are plenty of people,' he replied, 'who'll say you don't know where your honour lies. But since you're so reluctant to show me respect, you can take it that Bosi and I will share the same fate. I'll defend him as I would my own life, for as long as my courage lasts and till my dying day. Plenty of people will say that your bastard son was dearly bought if you decide to sacrifice us for his sake.'

Herraud was in a rage, and turned away. He didn't stop until he had found Bosi and told him what had happened between the king and himself.

Hring had the alarm sounded to call his forces together, and then he went against the foster-brothers. The fighting began at once. The king had twice or three times as many men as they had, and though Herraud and Bosi fought bravely and killed a good many men, they were over-powered in the end, and shackled and thrown into the dungeon. The king was so furious he wanted to have them killed there and then but Herraud was very well liked and everyone pleaded for his life. Then the booty was divided and the dead were buried. A number of people put it to the king that he ought to make peace with Herraud, and eventually Herraud was led before him. The king offered to spare his life, and many people spoke in favour of this, but Herraud refused the offer unless Bosi were spared as well. The king said that was out of the question. Herraud threatened to kill anyone who put Bosi to death, even the king himself. The king said it would serve Herraud right if he got the punishment he asked for. He was so angry no one could talk to him, and ordered Herraud to be taken back to the dungeon and the two men to be killed the following morning. The king was adamant, and it seemed to most people that the situation was quite hopeless.

That evening, Busla had a talk with her husband and asked him whether he wasn't going to offer some money for his son. Thvari answered that he'd no intention of throwing his money away, he knew only too well that he couldn't save the life of a man doomed soon to die. Then he asked Busla what had become of her magic if she wasn't going to give Bosi any help; but she said that she'd no intention of competing with Thvari in meanness.

That evening, Busla appeared in the king's bedroom and recited a prayer which has been known as 'Busla's Prayer' ever since. It has become famous everywhere, and contains many wicked words unfit for Christian mouths. This is how the prayer begins:

Here lies Hring,
Gotaland's king,
The stubbornest man
   when in the wrong:
He'll be the one
To kill his own son,
Beyond belief,
   yet on every tongue!

King, beware
Old Busla's prayer,
Soon it will echo
   through the world:
All who hear
Shall live in fear,
And into Hell
   your soul be hurled.

Demons will scatter,
All values shatter,

Cliffs will tremble
   to their knees:
Storms will batter,
Crash and clatter
Unless with Herraud
   you make your peace,
And let my Bosi
   live at ease.

Soon I shall dart
Close to your heart
With poison snakes
   to gnaw your breast:
Deafen your ears,
Blind you with tears,
Unless you let,
   my Bosi rest,
Embrace your son
   as an honoured guest.

When you set sail
May your rigging fail,
Your rudder-hooks snap
   in heavy seas:
The sheets will rip
On your sinking ship
Unless with Herraud
   you make your peace,
And let my Bosi
   live at ease.

When you ride, I'll make
Your bridle break,

Your horse go lame
    at my behest:
Straight from your door
To the demon's claw!
Unless you let
    my Bosi rest,
Embrace your son
    as an honoured guest.

You'll rest no more
Than on burning straw,
Your throne will be
Like a swollen sea;
And what a shame
When you play the game,
When she's on her back
But you've lost the knack:
Would you like some more . . .

'Shut your mouth, you filthy witch,' said the king, 'get out of here, or I'll have you tortured for your curses.'

'Now we're face to face,' said Busla, 'it's not likely that we'll part till I have what I came for.'

The king wanted to stand up, but he was stuck fast to the bed, and none of his servants could be roused from their sleep. Then Busla recited the second part of her prayer, but I'd better not write it here, as people repeat it only at their peril. If it's not written down, the prayer is less likely to be repeated. All the same, this is how it starts:

Sorceresses,
Elves and Trolls,
Goblins and giants

Will burn your halls:
Frost giants fright you
Stallions ride you,
Straws shall sting you,
Tempests bring you
To madness and Hell
If you break my spell.

When the second part was over, the king said to Busla, 'Rather than let you curse me any more, I'm going to let Herraud live. But Bosi must leave the country and if ever I lay hands on him I'll have him killed.'

'In that case, I'll have to deal with you further,' said Busla.

Then she started reciting the so-called 'Syrpa Verses' which hold the most powerful magic, and which nobody is allowed to sing after sunset. This stanza comes near the end:

Of strangers six
The names are here:
What they might mean
You must make clear:
Solve this riddle,
But if you fail
To satisfy me,
The dogs of Hell
Will tear your body
Bit by bit,
As your soul sinks down
To the burning pit.

ᚱ.ᚠ.ᚦ.ᚣ.ᚤ.ᚿ||||| ᚖᚖᚖᚖᚖᚖ : ᛏᛏᛏᛏᛏᛏ : |||||| : ᚱᚱᚱᚱᚱᚱ : *

'Interpret these names correctly or all my worst curses will bite you, unless you do as I ask,' she said.

When Busla had completed her prayer, the king had no idea how he ought to react to her demands. 'What do you want, then?' he asked.

'You're to send Bosi and Herraud on a dangerous mission,' said Busla, '– who knows how it will end – and they're to be responsible for their own safety.'

The king told her to go but she refused to leave until he'd given his solemn word to carry out his promises to her; and then, Busla's prayer could do him no harm.

After that the old hag went away.

BOSI'S MISSION

Early next morning the king got up and had the alarm sounded to call people to a meeting, and then Herraud and Bosi were led before the gathering. The king asked his counsellors what should be done with the two men, and most of them pleaded with him to spare Herraud.

Then the king spoke to his son. 'You don't seem inclined to show me much respect,' he said, 'but in spite of that I'm going to do as my friends ask me: I'm going to spare Bosi's life. He's to leave this country and not come back until he brings me a vulture's egg, inscribed all over with gold letters, and then we'll be reconciled. If not, everyone can call him a coward. Herraud is free to go wherever he wants to, either with Bosi or on any other path he chooses. After what's happened, I only want him to stay away from me.'

So the two men were set free. They went to Thvari and stopped with him over the winter. In the spring they got ready for a voyage with one ship and a crew of twenty-four. Mostly they let themselves be guided by Busla's advice. And so they set off and sailed east across the Baltic, and when they came to Permia they brought their ships in under cover of a thickly wooded wilderness.

A NIGHT IN THE WOOD

At that time the ruler of Permia was King Harek, a married man with two sons, Hrærek and Siggeir. They were great fighters, serving at the court of King Godmund of Glasir Plains, and they were also in charge of the country's defences. King Harek had a daughter called Edda, a beautiful girl, and very talented in most matters.

Now we must return to the foster-brothers, who were lying off Vina Forest in Permia where they'd set up a tent ashore in a remote and desolate spot.

One morning Bosi told his men he was going ashore with Herraud to explore the forest and see what they could find. 'Wait a month for us here, and if we're not back by then, you can sail wherever you like.' Their men weren't too happy about this, but there was nothing they could do about it.

The foster-brothers made their way into the wood. They had nothing to eat except what they could catch by shooting wild animals and birds; sometimes their only food was berries and the sap of the trees, and their clothes were badly torn by the branches.

One day they came upon a cottage. An old man was standing outside it splitting firewood, and he greeted them and asked who they were. They told him and asked him his name, and he said he was called Hoketil. Then he said they were welcome to stay the night if they wanted to, so they accepted his offer. The old man showed them to the living-room, where not many people were to be seen. The woman of the house was getting on in years, but there was an attractive young daughter. The girl pulled off their wet clothes and gave them dry things instead, then brought a basin so they could wash their hands. The table was laid, and the young woman served them with excellent ale. Bosi kept eyeing her suggestively and touching her foot with his toe, and she did the same to him.

In the evening they were shown to a comfortable bed. The farmer slept in a bed-closet, his daughter in the middle of the room and the foster-brothers in a bed under the gable beside the door. When the people were asleep, Bosi got up, went over to the young woman's bed and lifted the bedclothes off her. She asked who was there, and Bosi told her.

'What have you come for?' she asked.

'I wasn't comfortable enough in my bed as things were,'

he said, and added that he'd like to get under the bed-clothes with her.

'What do you want to do here?' she said.

'I want to temper my warrior,' said Bosi.

'What sort of warrior's that?' she asked.

'He's still very young and he's never been steeled,' he said, 'but a warrior ought to be hardened early on in life.'

He gave her a gold ring and got into bed beside her. She asked him where the warrior was, and he told her to feel between his legs, but she pulled her hand back and said he could keep his warrior and asked why he was carrying a monster like that on him, as hard as a tree. He told her the warrior would soften in the dark hole, and then she said he could do anything he wanted. So now he set the warrior between her legs. The path before him was rather narrow, and yet he managed to complete his mission.

After that they lay quiet for a while, as long as they pleased, and then the girl asked him if the tempering of the warrior had been a complete success. Bosi asked her in turn whether she felt like tempering him again, and she said she'd be only too pleased as long as he felt like it.

There's no record of how often they played the game that night, but it's believed that Bosi asked her, 'Have you any idea where I can find a vulture's egg inscribed with gold letters? My foster-brother and I have been sent to find out.'

She said the very least she could do in payment for the gold ring and a good night's entertainment was to tell him all he wanted to know.

'But who's so angry with you that he wants you to die, sending you on such a dangerous mission?'

'Evil motives aren't the only motives, and a man can't win a reputation without some effort,' said Bosi. 'Plenty of things seem full of danger to start with, but bring you luck in the end.'

THE VULTURE'S EGG

'In this forest,' said the girl, 'there's a great temple belonging to King Harek, the ruler of Permia. The god worshipped there is called Jomali, and a great quantity of gold and jewels can be found there, too. The king's mother, Kolfrosta, is in charge of the temple. Her witchcraft is so powerful that nothing could ever take her by surprise. By her sorcery she's been able to predict that she won't live out the month, so she's travelled by magic east to Glasir Plains and carried off King Godmund's sister, Hleid, whom she means to take her place as the priestess of the temple. But that would be a loss indeed – Hleid's one of the most beautiful and well-bred of women – so it would be all for the best if it could be prevented.'

'What's the main problem about the temple?' Bosi asked.

'An enormous vulture,' she said, 'so savage it destroys

everything that comes anywhere near it. The vulture watches the door and sees anything that comes inside. Not a living soul has a chance if the vulture's claws and venom come anywhere near him. Under this vulture lies the egg you've been sent to get. There's also a slave in the temple, who looks after the priestess's food – she eats a two-year-old heifer at every meal. And there's an enchanted demonic bull in the temple, shackled with iron chains. The bull's supposed to mount the heifer, poisoning her flesh, and then all those who taste it go crazy. The heifer is to be cooked for Hleid, and then she'll turn into a monster like the priestess. As things are, I don't think it's very likely you'll be able to beat these devils, considering all the sorcery you're up against.'

Bosi thanked her for telling him all this and repaid her handsomely with yet another round of good entertainment. They were both very pleased with themselves, and slept till dawn. In the morning, he went over to Herraud and repeated what he'd been told. They stayed on for another three nights, and then the farmer's daughter directed them to the temple. She wished them luck, and they set out on their journey.

Early one morning they saw a tall man in a grey cloak leading a cow. They realized this must be the slave, so they attacked him. Bosi struck him a heavy blow with a club, and that was the end of him. Then they killed the heifer and skinned her, and stuffed the hide with moss and heather. Herraud put on the slave's cloak and dragged the heifer's skin behind him. Bosi threw his cloak over the slave's body and carried him on his back. When they came in sight of the temple, Bosi took his spear and drove it into the slave's backside up through the body so that it jutted out of the shoulder. They walked up to the temple and, wearing the slave's clothes, Herraud went inside.

The priestess was asleep. Herraud led the heifer into the stall, then untied the bull, and the bull mounted the heifer at once. But the moss-filled hide collapsed on impact, so that the bull fell forward against the stone wall, breaking both its horns. Herraud gripped the bull by the ears and the jaw, and gave the neck such a violent twist that it broke. At that moment the priestess woke up and jumped to her feet.

Bosi walked into the temple carrying the slave over his head by the spear. The vulture wasted no time and dived down from the nest, intending to make a meal of this intruder, but it only swallowed the upper part of the corpse, and Bosi gave the spear a firm thrust so that it went straight through the vulture's throat into the heart. The vulture set its claws hard against the slave's buttocks and struck the tips of its wings against Bosi's ears, knocking him out. Then the vulture crashed down on top of him, ferocious in its death throes.

Herraud made for the priestess, and there was quite a tussle between them, as she wore her nails cut jagged and tore his flesh down to the bone. The fight took them to the spot where Bosi was lying, the floor around him soaked with blood. The priestess slipped in the vulture's blood and fell flat on her back, and so the struggle continued as fierce as ever, with Herraud sometimes on top of her and sometimes underneath.

Then Bosi came to, got hold of the bull's head and hit the old hag hard on the nose with it. Herraud tore one of her arms off at the shoulder, and after that her spirit began to weaken. Even so, her final death throes caused an earthquake.

After that they went through the temple and searched it thoroughly. In the vulture's nest they found the egg, covered in letters of gold. They found so much gold there they had more than enough to carry. Then they came to the altar where Jomali was sitting, and from him they took a gold crown set with twelve precious stones, and a necklace worth three hundred gold marks; and from his knees they took a silver cup filled with red gold and so big that four men couldn't drink it dry. The fine canopy that was hung over the god was more valuable than three cargoes of the richest merchantman that sails the Ægean Sea, and all this they took for themselves.

In the temple they found a secret side-room with a stone door, securely locked. It took them the whole day to break it open and get inside. There they saw a woman sitting on a chair – never had they seen such a beautiful woman! Her hair was tied to the chair-posts, and was as fair as polished straw or threads of gold. An iron chain, firmly locked, lay round her waist, and she was in tears.

When she saw the men, she asked them what had been causing all the uproar that morning. 'Do you care so little for your lives that you're willing to put yourselves into the power of demons? The masters of this place will kill you the moment they see you here.'

They said there'd be plenty of time to talk about that later. Then they asked her what her name was, and why she was being treated so badly. She said her name was Hleid and that she was the sister of King Godmund of Glasir Plains in the east.

'The ogress in charge here got hold of me by magic, and wants me to become priestess here when she's dead and take over the sacrifice in the temple. But I'd rather be burnt alive.'

'You'd be good to the man who helped you escape from here?' asked Herraud. She said she didn't think anyone could possibly manage that.

'Will you marry me if I take you away?' asked Herraud.

'I don't know a man on earth so loathsome I'd not prefer being married to him rather than worshipped in this temple,' she said. 'What's your name?'

'I'm called Herraud,' he said, 'and my father is King Hring of East Gotaland. You needn't worry any more about the priestess. Bosi and I have already given her a good send-off. But you understand, I feel entitled to some reward from you if I get you out of this place.'

'I've nothing to offer but myself,' she said, 'that is, if my family will let me.'

'I don't intend to ask them,' said Herraud, 'and I won't have any more evasion, since it seems to me that I'm every bit as good as you. So whatever you decide, I'll set you free.'

'Of all the men I ever set eyes on, there's no one I'd rather have than you,' she said.

Then they set her free. Herraud asked what she would prefer, to travel home with them and become his wife; or else to be sent east to her brother, never to see Herraud again. She chose to go with him, and so they pledged themselves to each other.

They carried the gold and treasures out of the temple and then set fire to the building and burned it to ashes so that there was nothing else to be seen there. After that they set off with all that they'd taken and didn't break their journey till they reached Hoketil's house. Nor did they stay there very long, but gave him a great deal of money, then carried the gold and treasure on a number of horses down to the ship.

Their men were delighted to see them.

THE BATTLE OF BROW PLAINS

They sailed away from Permia as soon as the wind was in their favour, and there's nothing to tell of their voyage until they arrived back home in Gotaland, having been away two years. They went before the king, and Bosi delivered the egg. The shell had cracked, but even the broken piece was worth ten gold marks. The king used the shell as a loving-cup. Bosi also gave him the silver cup that he'd taken from Jomali and now they were completely reconciled.

About this time the queen's brothers, Dayfarer and Nightfarer, came to the royal court. They had been sent by King Harald Wartooth to ask for support, as a time had been set for the Battle of Brow Plains. This battle was the greatest ever fought in Scandinavia, and is described in the Saga of Sigurd Hring, father of Ragnar Hairy-Breeks.

Meanwhile, Hring asked Herraud to go in his place, and offered to look after the bride. He also said that he and Herraud should be fully reconciled over all that had happened between them. Herraud did as his father asked. He and Bosi joined the brothers with five hundred men and went to King Harald. In this battle King Harald and one hundred and fifteen other kings were killed, as it says in his Saga, and many great champions as well, even greater men than the kings themselves. Both Dayfarer and Nightfarer were killed. Herraud and Bosi were wounded but managed to come out of the battle alive.

Meanwhile in Gotaland great changes had taken place while they were away, as will soon be told.

THE DEATH OF HRING

Since it's not feasible to tell more than one story at a time, we'd now better explain what had happened earlier on. We begin at the point where King Godmund's sister, Hleid, had vanished from Glasir Plains. As soon as the king realized she had disappeared, he had a search made for her by sea and land, but no one could find any trace of her. The two brothers, Hrærek and Siggeir, were staying with the king at the time. The king asked Siggeir to take charge of the search for Hleid, and as a reward he was to win her for his wife. Siggeir said that in his opinion Hleid would be very hard to trace, unless the priestess in Permia knew where she was. The brothers prepared to sail with five ships. When they reached Permia, they found King Harek and told him about their mission. He advised them to go to the temple, and said that if neither the god Jomali nor the priestess knew Hleid's whereabouts, there wasn't much hope of finding her. The brothers went to the temple and saw nothing but a vast heap of ashes, with not a sign of anything that should have been there.

The brothers scoured the forest until they came upon Hoketil's house. They asked if he or his household had any idea who could have destroyed the temple. The old man said he didn't know, but he mentioned that two men from Gotaland had been lying at anchor for a long time off Vina Forest, one called Herraud and the other Bosi. In his opinion they were the most likely men to have done such an extraordinary thing. The farmer's daughter said she had seen these men on their way to the ship, bringing King Godmund's sister with them, Hleid of Glasir Plains. They had told the girl that anyone who wanted to see Hleid should come to them.

When the brothers learned what had happened, they told the king, then gathered forces all over Permia, and with twenty-three ships they sailed to Gotaland. They arrived there about the time of the Battle of Brow Plains where the foster-brothers were fighting, so Hring had only a small force with him. Hrærek and Siggeir told him either to fight or else hand over Hleid to them. The king chose rather to fight, but the matter was soon settled as Hring and the greater part of his army were killed.

Then the brothers took the girl, stole all the money they could and sailed back without delay to Glasir Plains. King Godmund was delighted to get his sister back and thanked them generously for their mission, which was considered a great success. Siggeir made a proposal of marriage to Hleid, but she was unhappy and said it would be more fitting if she were to marry the man who had saved her from the monsters.

The king said that Siggeir fully deserved to have her and added that he himself was the one to settle her marriage. 'And no foreign princes are going to have you, even if you won't accept my decision.' So she had to do as the king wished.

And now we'd better let them get on with their wedding preparations, since they are looking forward to them so much, though it may happen yet that the feast won't go without a hitch.

BOSI'S ADVENTURES

Now we should explain that Herraud and Bosi arrived home in Gotaland a fortnight after Siggeir and his men had sailed away. Their return was a great sadness to them, but they took stock of the situation and then Bosi went to his father to ask for advice. Thvari said there was no time to gather a whole army and the only way of rescuing Hleid was by means of carefully laid plans and swift action, so the outcome was that they prepared a single ship with thirty men aboard. It was decided that Smid should go with them and be in charge of the expedition. Thvari gave them plenty of sound advice, and so did Busla.

They set off as soon as they were ready. Smid always had a favourable wind whenever he was at the helm, so their voyage was much faster than anyone might have expected. Soon the brothers had reached Glasir Plains in the east. They cast anchor off a thickly wooded coast, and Smid threw a helmet of invisibility over the ship.

Herraud and Bosi went ashore and came to a small well-kept cottage. An old man was living there with his wife, and they had an attractive and well-informed daughter. The peasant gave them an invitation to stay the night, which they accepted. The cottage was quite comfortable, and the hospitality good. The table was laid, and the guests were served with excellent beer. The master of the house was silent and reserved, but his daughter, the most sociable member of the household, was the one who served the guests. Bosi was in a good humour and flirted with her a little, and she did the same with him.

In the evening they were shown to their beds, but as soon as the light had been put out, Bosi went over to the girl and lifted the bedclothes off her. She asked who was there, and Bosi told her.

'What do you want?' she asked.

'I'd like to water my colt at your wine-spring,' he said.

'Do you think you can manage it, my lad?' she asked. 'He's hardly used to a well like mine.'

'I'll lead him right to the edge, then push him in if there's no other way to make him drink,' said Bosi.

'Where is your colt, sweetheart?' she asked.

'Between my legs, love,' he said. 'You can touch him, but do it gently, he's terribly shy.'

She took hold of his prick, and stroked it and said, 'It's a lively colt, though his neck is far too straight.'

'His head isn't all that well set,' agreed Bosi, 'but his neck curves much better once he's had a drink.'

'Well, it's all up to you now,' she said.

'Lie as open as you can,' said Bosi, 'and keep calm.'

Then he watered his colt generously, completely immersing him. This pleased the girl so much she was hardly able to speak. 'Are you sure you're not drowning the colt?' she asked.

'He has to be given all he can possibly take,' said Bosi, 'he often gives me a lot of trouble when he isn't allowed to drink his fill.'

Bosi kept at it for as long as he wanted, then took a rest. The girl was wondering where all the fluid between her legs had come from, for the whole bed was lathering under her.

'Could it be your colt's drunk more than was good for

him,' she asked, 'and then vomited up more than he's drunk?'

'Something's the matter with him,' said Bosi, 'he's as soft as a lung.'

'He's probably ale-sick,' she said, 'like any drunkard.'

'Could be,' he said.

So they entertained themselves to their satisfaction, the girl being now under him and now on top. She said she'd never ridden a more even-paced colt than this.

After many an entertaining turn, she asked him who he was. He told her and in turn asked her what was the latest news in the land. The very latest news, she replied, was that the brothers Siggeir and Hrærek had got back the King's sister, Hleid, from Gotaland and killed Hring.

'It's gained them such a reputation that no one here in the east can measure up to them,' she said. 'The king has promised his sister Hleid to Siggeir against her wishes, and the wedding is to be in three days' time. The brothers are very much on their guard, they've spies on every road and at every harbour. It's impossible to take them by surprise. They're expecting Herraud and Bosi to come at any time to fetch Hleid. The king has had a hall built, so huge there's a hundred doors in it, with the same distance between each of them, and a hundred men can sit in every space. There are two watchmen at every door, and no one is allowed to pass through unless he's been vouched for by one of the doorkeepers. Those who aren't recognized at any of the doors are to be kept in the dungeons until it's known who they are. There's a raised bed standing in the middle of the floor of the hall, with four steps leading up to it. The bride and bridegroom are to lie there, and all the retainers will be keeping watch round the bed, so it's impossible to catch them unawares.'

'Which of the retainers is the king's favourite?' asked Bosi.

'He's called Sigurd,' she said, 'the king's counsellor. He's a master-musician, there's nobody to compare with him anywhere, particularly at playing the harp. Just now Sigurd's visiting his concubine, a peasant's daughter living near the forest. She makes his clothes while he tunes his instruments.'

After that they dropped the subject and slept for the rest of the night.

A WEDDING FEAST

Early in the morning Bosi went back to Herraud and told him what he'd learnt during the night. They got ready to leave, and Bosi gave the young woman a gold ring. They followed her instructions about which way they should go, until they came in sight of the farm where Sigurd was staying. Then they saw him making for the royal palace with a servant. The foster-brothers stepped forward into their path. Bosi drove his spear through Sigurd, and Herraud strangled the servant. Afterwards, Bosi flayed the bodies. Then they went back to the ship, told Smid what they had done, and between them settled their plans.

Smid put Sigurd's clothes and the skin of his face on Bosi, and wore the other mask and the servant's outfit himself.

Then they told Herraud what he had to do and walked up to the palace. They came up to the door where King Godmund was waiting, and he thought this was Sigurd, so he welcomed him and led him into the palace. 'Sigurd' took charge of the royal coffers, and of the ale supplies and wine cellars, too. It was he who decided what ale should be served first, and told the cup-bearers how generously they were to serve the drinks. He said it was most important that the guests should get as drunk as possible on the first night of the feast, since in that way they would stay drunk much longer.

All the important guests were shown to their seats, and the bride was escorted into the palace and led to her bench with a large company of elegant young women.

King Godmund sat on the high-seat. Beside him sat the bridegroom with Hrærek in attendance on him. It isn't said how the other noblemen were placed, but this much is known, that 'Sigurd' played the harp before the bride and her maidens. When the toasts were being served, 'Sigurd' played so well, everyone remarked that he had no equal, but he said this was only the beginning. The king told him not to spare his efforts. When the memorial cup consecrated to Thor was carried into the hall, 'Sigurd' changed the tune. Then everything loose began to move – knives, plates and anything else which no one was holding on to – and lots of people jumped up from their seats and danced on the floor. This went on for quite some time.

Next came the toast dedicated to all the gods. 'Sigurd' changed the tune again, and this time he played so loud, the music rang through the entire palace. All the people inside jumped to their feet, except the king and the bridal couple. All the guests were shuffling about and so was everything else inside the hall. This too went on for quite some time.

The king asked whether 'Sigurd' knew any more tunes. He answered that there were still a few less important ones and advised everybody to take a rest for a while. The guests sat down and carried on with their drinking. Then he played the tunes of the 'Ogress', the 'Dreamer' and the 'Warrior', and after that it was time for Odin's toast to be drunk. Then 'Sigurd' opened the harp. It was heavily inlaid with gold, and so big that a man could stand upright inside it. From inside he took a pair of white gloves, gold-embroidered, and played the 'Coif-Thrower'. Then all the coifs were blown off the ladies' heads, and danced above the crossbeams in the hall. All the men and women jumped to their feet, and not a thing remained still in its place.

When Odin's toast had been drunk, there was only one more left, the toast dedicated to Freyja. Then 'Sigurd' started plucking the one string that lies across the other strings, and told the king to get ready for the tune called 'Powerful'. The king was so startled at this tune that he jumped to his feet and the bride and bridegroom too, and nobody danced more vigorously than they did. This went on for quite some time. Now Smid took the bride by the hand, led her a lively dance, and when he got the chance, picked up the table service and bundled it into the bridal sheets.

Now we come back to Herraud, who told his men to stave in all the ships along the coast, making them unseaworthy. He sent some others up to the town to collect the gold and jewels that Smid had put ready for them to carry down to the sea. By now it was growing very dark. Some of the men were on the roof of the palace, watching what was happening inside and hauling up through the skylight what had been thrown into the sheets. Others carried this down to the ship, which had been pointed out to sea.

ABDUCTION

The next thing to happen was this. While the people in the palace were having their fling, a stranger walked inside, a tall, handsome man wearing a red scarlet tunic, with a silver belt round his waist and a gold band on his forehead. He was unarmed and started dancing like the others. When he came before the high-seat, he raised his fist and punched the king so hard on the nose that three teeth shot out of his mouth. Blood began to pour from the king's nose and mouth, and he fell unconscious on to the floor.

'Sigurd' saw what had happened, and threw the harp into the bed. Then he struck the stranger with both fists between the shoulder-blades. The man turned away, with 'Sigurd' after him. A good many followed, while others were attending to the king. Now 'Sigurd' took the bride by the hand, led her up to the bed and locked her inside the harp, and the men on the roof hauled her and Smid up through the skylight. After that they hurried down to the ship and went on board. The man who had hit the king was already there before them. 'Sigurd' stepped aboard as soon as he arrived, but Siggeir was right behind him with sword in hand. Then 'Sigurd' turned to face him and pushed him into the sea. Siggeir's men had to fish him out of the water, more dead than alive.

Smid cut the moorings, and the crew set sail. They tried to reach open water as fast as possible by rowing and sailing at the same time. Hrærek rushed down to the beach with a number of other men to launch their ships, but the coal-black sea poured in, and they had to make their way back to the shore. There was in fact nothing much they could do about it, as all of them were helplessly drunk.

The king was very shaky when he came to. He was offered some food, but he was still too weak to take any. The festivities had turned sour and sorry. Still, when the king had recovered, they made their plans. They decided not to disband but get themselves ready as quickly as they could to chase after the foster-brothers.

While they are busy getting ready, we must take up the

story of the others. They sailed on their way till they came to the point where one route lies to Gotaland and the other to Permia. Then Bosi told Herraud to sail on to Gotaland and said he himself had some business in Permia.

Herraud said he was not going to leave him. 'What's your business there anyway?' he asked.

Bosi said this would become clear later. Smid offered to wait for them five days, and Bosi said that would be long enough. Then the two men rowed ashore in a small boat and hid it in a secret cove. They walked for a while until they came to a house belonging to an old man and his wife, who had a good-looking daughter. The foster-brothers were given a friendly welcome and served with excellent wine in the evening.

Bosi gave the girl a cheerful smile, and she eyed him in return. A little later they all went to sleep. Bosi went over to her bed, and she asked what he wanted. He said he wanted her to put a ring on his stump. She said she wondered what ring he could be talking about, and he asked her didn't she have one? She answered that she hadn't any ring that would fit him.

'I can widen it if it's too narrow,' he said.

'Where's that stump of yours? I've got a fair idea of what I can expect from my narrow little ring.'

He told her to feel between his legs, but she pulled her hand back and said he could keep his stump.

'What does it remind you of?' he asked.

'My father's steel-yard with the ring broken off.'

'You're very critical,' said Bosi. He took a ring off his finger and gave it her. She asked what he wanted in return.

'I want to put a stopper in your bung-hole,' he said.

'I can't think what you mean,' she said.

'Lie as open as you can,' he said.

She did as he asked, and he went between her legs and made a thrust deep into her body, almost up under her ribs.

She gave a jump, and said, 'You've pushed the stopper right through the hole, man.'

'I'll get it out again,' he said. 'How did you like that?'

'Nice as a drink of fresh mead,' she said. 'Keep the mop stirring in the flue.'

He kept nothing back, and she got so warmed up she began to feel a bit sick, so she asked him to leave off, and they took a rest. Then she asked him who he was, and he told her. He asked her whether she was by any chance on friendly terms with the king's daughter, Edda. She answered that she often visited Edda's boudoir and was always given a good welcome there.

'I'll take you into my confidence,' he said. 'I'm going to give you three marks of silver and, in return, you get the princess to join me in the wood.'

Then he took three walnuts from his purse, as bright as gold, and gave them to her. She was to tell the princess that she knew a grove in the forest where walnuts like these were plentiful.

The girl warned him that the princess wouldn't be afraid of just one man. 'There's a eunuch called Skalk who goes everywhere with her, and he's as strong as twelve men, and ready for anything.'

Bosi said he didn't mind as long as the odds were no worse.

Early next morning the girl went to see the princess, showed her the golden walnuts and told her she knew a place where they were plentiful.

'Let's go there right away and take Skalk with us,' said the princess, and that's what they did.

Bosi and Herraud were already in the grove and met them there. Bosi greeted the great lady and asked her why she was travelling with so small a retinue. She said there was no risk involved.

'That's what you think,' said Bosi. 'Now make your choice: either come with me willingly, or I'll make you my wife right now, here in the wood.'

The eunuch asked who the ruffian was that dared to mouth on like that. Herraud told him to shut up and not behave like an idiot. The eunuch hit out at Herraud with a heavy cudgel, and Herraud parried it with his shield, but it was such a powerful blow that the shield was shattered. Herraud rushed at Skalk but he gave a good account of himself. There was a hard tussle between them, but Skalk wouldn't budge an inch. Then Bosi came up to them and pulled Skalk's feet from under him. After that they put a noose round his neck and hanged him on an oak tree.

Then Bosi took the princess and carried her in his arms down to the shore where they rowed out to the ship and found Smid. The princess took it badly, but after Smid had had a few words with her she soon cheered up.

And so they sailed back home to Gotaland.

A BATTLE

While all this was going on, Siggeir and Hrærek had gathered and fitted out a huge army, but King Godmund was unfit to travel because of the punch Herraud had given him, so the brothers were in sole charge. They set off from Glasir Plains with forty ships, but added a good many more as they went along. They went to Permia to see their father, King Harek, just after Bosi and Herraud had left. By now King Harek knew for certain that the foster-brothers had gone off with his daughter. He had his own forces ready with fifteen large ships, so he joined his sons on their expedition, and between them they had sixty ships in all, and with this fleet they sailed to Gotaland.

Now we come back to Herraud and Bosi, who had begun to gather forces as soon as they arrived home, as they wanted to be ready in case they were being followed, though they meant to celebrate the double wedding as soon as they had the time and the opportunity. While they were away Thvari had had a lot of spears, axes and arrows made, and now the army began to grow.

When they heard that King Harek and his sons were approaching the coast, and things didn't look so good, Herraud ordered ships to be launched to meet them. He had a large force of hand-picked men, but it was much smaller than King Harek's. Smid attacked the king's ship, while Bosi went for Hrærek, and Herraud for Siggeir. There's no need to go into detail over what happened next. A fierce battle broke out, with both sides eager for action.

Shortly after the battle had begun, Siggeir boarded Herraud's ship and soon killed one of his men. Herraud had a forecastleman called Snidil, and he threw a spear at Siggeir, who caught it in flight and hurled it back at him. The spear went right through Snidil and into the prow, pinning him fast to the timbers. Herraud turned to meet Siggeir and lunged at him with a halberd. It broke through his shield but Siggeir gave it a powerful tug so that Herraud lost hold of the weapon. At the same time Siggeir hit back at Herraud, slicing off his ear and part of his helmet. Herraud picked up a great log that was lying on the deck and hit him on the nose, knocking the visor off the helmet and breaking his nose and all his teeth. Siggeir tumbled backwards into his own ship, and lay there unconscious for some time.

Smid fought bravely, but King Harek managed to board his ship with eleven men and they caused a lot of damage. Then Smid turned to meet him and lunged at him with a special short-sword that Busla had given him, since Harek couldn't be hurt by ordinary weapons. The blow caught him in the face, breaking all his teeth and cutting his palate and lips. Blood poured out of his mouth. This blow so upset King Harek that he turned into a flying dragon and spewed venom all over the ship, killing a number of men, then dived down at Smid and swallowed him in one gulp.

Next, they saw an enormous bird, called *skergipr*, flying down from the land. This bird had a nasty big head and it's often compared with the devil himself. The bird attacked the dragon, and a savage battle began. Eventually, they both came plunging down, the *skergipr* crashing into the sea and the dragon on to Siggeir's ship. Herraud was already there, letting fly with the log on either hand. He struck Siggeir on the ear, cracking his skull and knocking him overboard, and he never came up after that.

Then King Harek came to and transformed himself into a boar. He snapped at Herraud with his teeth, tore the mail-coat off his body and bit into his breast, ripping off both nipples and all the flesh down to the bare bone. Herraud struck at the boar's snout, cutting clean through the head below the eyes. Herraud was now so exhausted that he collapsed on his back. The boar trampled on him but wasn't able to bite him as its snout had been cut off.

Next a monstrous bitch with enormous teeth appeared on the deck. She tore a hole into the boar's groin, unravelled his guts and jumped overboard. Harek reappeared in human form and dived into the sea after her. Both sank to the bottom of the sea and never came up again. It's commonly believed that this bitch would have been Busla, since after that she was never seen again.

By this time Bosi had boarded Hrærek's ship and was fighting like a true hero. Then he saw his father floating in the water just beside the ship, so he dived in and helped him aboard his own ship.

Hrærek was already aboard and had killed a good many men. Bosi was exhausted when he climbed aboard, but in spite of that he turned on Hrærek and hewed at his shield, splitting it in two and cutting off his leg at the ankle. The sword finished up in the yard-arm and broke in two. Hrærek hit back and struck at Bosi as he was turning. The sword caught him on the helmet and ran down on to the shoulder, ripping the mail-coat and wounding him in the shoulder-blade, and so right down his back. All his clothes were torn off so he stood there stark naked with the heel-bone sliced off his left foot. Bosi then seized a piece of the yard-arm, but Hrærek tried to jump overboard. He was leaning against the bulwark when Bosi struck at him, severing the body so that one part fell overboard and the other into the ship. By this time most of the enemy had been killed, but those still alive were spared.

The foster-brothers now took a roll-call of their troops. No more than a hundred were in any condition to fight, but they had won a great victory, and now they shared out what they had taken in the battle, and gave treatment to all the wounded who could benefit from it.

After that Herraud and Bosi made arrangements for their weddings. There was no shortage of anything that was needed, and the feast lasted a month. When it was over, they gave all the guests splendid parting gifts. Herraud became king of all the territories his father had once ruled.

A little later they gathered their forces and went to Permia. Bosi demanded to be accepted as king there, since his wife Edda was legal heir to her father. Bosi told the people that this would be the best way of compensating the country for the men he had killed, that he could make them strong, with better laws and greater justice, and that since they now had no leader, the best solution would be to make him their king. Edda was well known to them and they knew all about her qualities, so Bosi became the king of Permia.

Bosi had a son by the girl who had tempered his warrior for him. He was called Svidi the Bold, and his son was Vilmund the Absentminded.

Bosi went east to Glasir Plains and made peace between King Godmund and Herraud.

Herraud and Hleid loved each other dearly, and their daughter was Thora Town-Hart, who married Ragnar Hairy-Breeks.

According to legend, a small snake was found in the vulture's egg which Herraud and Bosi had fetched from Permia. It was golden in colour, and King Herraud gave it to his daughter as a teething-gift. She put a piece of gold under the snake, and after that it grew and grew until it circled her bower. The snake was so savage no one dared come near it except the king and the man who fed it. The snake ate an old ox at every meal, and everyone thought it a thoroughly nasty creature. King Herraud made a solemn vow that he would only marry Thora to the man brave enough to go into the bower and destroy the snake, but no one had enough courage for this until Ragnar, son of Sigurd Hring, appeared on the scene. This Ragnar has since been known as Ragnar Hairy-Breeks, and his nickname is taken from the clothes he had made for himself when he went to kill the snake.

And so we end the Saga of Stunt-Bosi.

Egil and Asmund

BRYNHILD

There was a king called Hertrygg who ruled over Russia, a large, well-populated country lying between Hunland and Novgorod. He was married and had two daughters, both called Hild. They were fine-looking, even-tempered girls, very well brought-up, and the king was extremely fond of them.

Once when the king was away on a hunting trip, the elder Hild went with her maidens to a nut-grove. She was called Brynhild, because she had been trained in the skills of knighthood. As the women were getting ready to return home from the wood, a huge beast, called the *hjasi*, came up to them. This is an enormous, savage creature and of all the beasts the *hjasi* has the longest life, which explains the saying that a very old man is 'as old as the *hjasi*'; it's shaped like a monstrous dog, but with ears so large they touch the ground. The women scattered in all directions as soon as they saw the creature, but the *hjasi* got hold of the princess and ran into the wood with her.

The maidens went back home and told what had happened. The king was terribly distressed by the news and had a search made for his daughter, but they could find no trace of her anywhere. No one could tell him anything about her disappearance, and soon people began to lose interest in it.

So time passed till Christmas.

At Christmas the king held a magnificent feast. The younger Hild, a clever girl – they called her Bekkhild because of her skill at embroidery – used to sit in her boudoir. On the first day of Christmas the king sent for his daughter, who made herself ready and went into the street with her maidens escorted by some gentlemen of the court. As they were passing a certain garden they heard a great uproar and saw a terrible vulture flying overhead. Its wings seemed to extend over the entire city. Then a great darkness fell and the vulture grabbed the princess and flew away with her. It struck two of her servants dead, and all the others were shaken with terror.

The news soon reached the royal palace. The king was extremely distressed and said, 'There seems no end to our misfortunes. I don't see what can be behind these monsters. I want you all to know that anyone who cares to search for my daughters shall not only marry one if he finds them, but get a third of my kingdom as well. Even if the searcher finds them dead, he can still have the best earldom in the country and choose any woman he wants as his wife.'

Some people called this a generous offer but added that there was a great deal at stake. After Christmas everyone went back home, deeply disturbed by what had happened.

Winter passed, and summer after. Late in the autumn it came about that a small ship, gold-painted above the water-line, put into the harbour with thirty men aboard, not including servants. The king happened to be at the harbour, and these men went before him to present themselves. He responded in a friendly way to their greetings and asked who they were. Their leader replied that his name was Asmund and that he was known as the Berserks-Killer.

'How old are you?' said the king.

'Sixteen,' said Asmund.

'I've never seen a more useful-looking fellow for your age,' said the king. 'Where have you come from?'

'A viking expedition,' said Asmund. 'But now winter's coming on and we'd like to have sanctuary here till spring. We're not short of money to pay our own way.'

The king said he was welcome to stay on, so Asmund had his cargo unloaded, and they were given a fine house to store their goods. Asmund, however, spent most of the time drinking in the king's palace. He and his men got on well with everybody.

EGIL ONE-HAND

One day after Asmund had been staying there a month it happened that eighteen men came into the hall, every one of them wounded. Their leader, Rognvald, was in charge of the king's defences. The king responded warmly to his greetings and asked who had given him such a rough handling.

'There's a man called Egil come to your country,' said Rognvald, 'a hard man to deal with. He's been plundering your kingdom, so I went against him with five well-equipped ships, while he had just one ship and a crew of thirty. I didn't expect them to give me any trouble but the outcome of the battle was that I had to run for it, and all my men have been killed, apart from those here. He only has a single hand, and so he's known as Egil One-Hand, but he manages to do more with the one that's missing than with the other. Just above the wrist there's a sword fixed, made by dwarfs, and there isn't a man alive can stand up to his strokes.'

With that Rognvald went to his seat and dropped down dead. 'The thought that your death won't be avenged is not to be borne,' said the king.

'The best way to repay your hospitality,' said Asmund, 'would be if I went to see this Egil.'

'I'd like that,' said the king. 'You can take as many men as you want.'

'I'm not in the habit of taking on extra men when the odds are fair,' said Asmund. 'But if Egil has more men than I have, the farmers are sure to help us.'

THE ENCOUNTER

Asmund set off to meet Egil, and told his men to row fully armed over to Egil's ship. Egil wasn't unprepared for this, and asked who was responsible for all that rowing.

47

Asmund gave his name. 'I've some business with you,' he added.

'Let's hear what you want,' said Egil.

'I want to exchange weapons with you,' said Asmund, 'and give you swords for axes.'

'We're not likely to refuse your offer,' said Egil. 'Do you have plenty of money aboard?'

Asmund said he hadn't. 'We're hoping to put that right with your help. How do you plan to compensate the king for your plunderings?'

'We're not in the habit of paying out money for the odd sheep my lads take for the table,' said Egil.

'In that case we'll have to use force,' said Asmund. 'The king's sent me for your head.'

'He must be pretty anxious to get rid of you,' said Egil. 'Why shouldn't we become sworn-brothers? Then we can kill the king and marry his daughters.'

'They're not available at the moment, they've both been abducted,' said Asmund.

'It would be a pity if our men were to kill each other,' said Egil. 'Let's fight a duel instead.'

Asmund said he was ready enough for that, so they went ashore to try out each other's skill, and were just about evenly matched. In the evening they all sat down to a joint drinking feast, and after that they slept through the night.

Next morning Asmund and Egil took up their weapons again and set to, each destroying three of the other's shields.

When the sun was due south, Egil said, 'Do you want to go on with the game?'

'Nothing's been proved either way yet,' said Asmund, 'and the king isn't going to think my mission's been properly carried out if we stop now.'

'Just as you wish,' said Egil.

'How old are you?' asked Asmund.

'Eighteen,' said Egil.

'Pick up your weapons if you want to live longer,' said Asmund.

So they fought another round, and it seemed to them as if every stroke was a death-blow. When the sun was in the south-west, Egil said, 'I think it would be better for us to stop this game now.'

'You must be getting scared,' said Asmund, who had already received one wound.

'Look out for yourself then,' said Egil.

So they fought the third round. Asmund could do no more than defend his life, and he'd already been wounded three times. He realized that this wouldn't do, so he threw down his sword and flung himself at Egil. It was difficult for Egil to use the mutilated hand, and the scuffle took them all over the field. At last Egil fell, and by then each had torn off the other's helmet.

'My sword's not to hand,' said Asmund, 'and it's too much trouble to bite your throat.'

'You've not much choice in the matter,' said Egil.

'I'm going to take a chance,' said Asmund, and ran for his sword and then back to Egil who lay as still as if he was having his hair cut.

Asmund said, 'You haven't any equal, Egil. Now stand

up. I want to accept the offer you made, and become your sworn-brother.'

'It worries me a lot,' said Egil, 'that I owe you my life.'

'I'm not going to kill you,' said Asmund, 'but I want you to come with me to the king.'

Then their men arrived on the scene and pleaded with them to be reconciled. So they shook hands and each agreed to become the other's sworn-brother according to ancient custom.

EAGLE-BEAK

They got ready for the voyage and went back to King Hertrygg. Asmund greeted the king, who received him kindly and asked if he had met Egil One-Hand.

Asmund said he certainly had. 'I've never met a braver man. He's offered to take Rognvald's place, and we'll defend your country together.'

'If you're both willing to swear an oath of loyalty and take his place, I'll accept this offer as a settlement,' said the king.

Asmund said he was willing to do that, then Egil was called for, and they were put in charge of the country's defences, and stayed there over winter.

At Christmas the king gave a feast, and on the first day he asked whether anyone there could tell him what had happened to his daughters, but no one could. Then the king repeated the offer he had made before.

Egil said, 'This is a chance for a brave man to earn some money.'

After Christmas all the guests returned home.

Soon after midwinter Egil and Asmund launched their ship and selected a crew of twenty-four. They put a man called Viglogi in charge of those who were left behind. Egil and Asmund announced that they were not coming back till they had found the king's daughters, dead or alive. Then they put to sea, though they had no idea of where they should go. They spent the summer exploring outlying islands, skerries and mountains, and by the autumn they had reached as far north as Jotunheim. There they sailed close in by a forest, hauled their ship ashore and made themselves comfortable.

The foster-brothers told their men to stay there over the winter. 'Egil and I are going to explore this country,' said Asmund, 'and if we don't come back next summer, you're free to go wherever you like.'

They set off into the wood, shooting wild animals and birds for food. But months passed by, and sometimes they had no food at all. One day they came to a valley with a river flowing through it and low grassy banks on either side. The hillsides were wooded below and rocky higher up. There they saw a large number of she-goats and some well-fed males. They rounded up the herd and got hold of one of the fat goats with the idea of slaughtering it. Then they heard shouting up the slope, all the goats scattered, and they lost hold of the one they'd caught. They saw a monster up among the rocks, broader than it was high. It spoke in a shrill, bell-like voice and asked who was so bold that he dared steal one of the queen's goats.

'Who are you, oh beautiful, bed-worthy lady? Where's your queen's country?'

'My name's Skin-Beak,' she said, 'I'm the daughter of Queen Eagle-Beak who rules over Jotunheim. Her residence isn't very far from here, and you'd better go and see her before you start stealing things.'

'You're absolutely right,' said Asmund, and gave her a gold ring.

'I daren't accept this,' she said, 'I'm sure my mother will say that's my bed-money.'

'I'm not in the habit of taking back my gifts,' said Asmund, 'but we'd like you to find us a place to stay.'

She went ahead of them home to her mother, who asked her why she was so late. Skin-Beak said she had found two men who needed hospitality. 'One of them gave me a gold ring and asked me to find them lodgings,' she said.

'Why did you take money from them?'

'I was hoping you might repay them for it,' said Skin-Beak.

'Why didn't you invite them here?'

'I wasn't sure how you'd take it.'

'Ask them over,' said Eagle-Beak.

Skin-Beak ran back to them and said, 'My mother wants you to come and see her. You'd better be ready with the news, because she's very sharp about most things.'

So they went to see the old hag. She asked them their names, and they told her. She could hardly take her eyes off Egil. They said they'd not eaten for a whole week. The hag was skimming the milk. She had fifty goats yielding as much as cows, and an enormous cauldron, big enough to hold all this milk. She had a vast wheat-field too, and every day she took from it so much meal that the gruel she made with it filled the cauldron, and this was the food she and her daughter lived on.

'Skin-Beak,' she said, 'you'd better get some brushwood and make a good fire. Our hospitality wouldn't be up to much if we only offered them gruel to eat.'

Skin-Beak wasted no time, but even so her mother told her to hurry up and serve the food that was already cooked. So some game and venison appeared on the table.

The hag said, 'Let's not sit around with nothing to say, even though the hospitality does leave something to be desired. It'll be a long while before the gruel's ready. Now, Asmund, you can tell us the story of your life, and then Egil can tell us his. After that I'll entertain you at table with some stories about my own adventures. I'm curious to hear about your family background and the reason for your travels.'

Asmund began his story: There was a king called Ottar who ruled over Halogaland. He was married to Sigrid, daughter of Earl Ottar of Jutland in Denmark, and they had a son called Asmund. He was a fine big fellow, and while he was still young he was trained in all kinds of skills. When he was twelve he was considered a better man than any in the land.

Asmund had a good many playmates. One day they'd gone riding into the forest, Asmund saw a hare and set his hounds on it. The hare ran away and the hounds couldn't catch it, but Asmund didn't give up, and when his horse collapsed from exhaustion Asmund ran with the hounds after the hare. In the end the hare jumped off a sea-cliff. Asmund turned back to look for his horse but he couldn't find it. Dusk had already fallen, so Asmund had to spend the night there, but in the morning a heavy mist had risen and he had no idea where he was.

For three days Asmund was completely lost in the wood, but then he saw someone coming towards him, a tall, handsome man, with a fine head of yellow silken hair, and wearing a scarlet cloak. It seemed to Asmund that he'd never seen a finer-looking man. They greeted each other, and Asmund asked the stranger's name. He said he was called Aran, the son of King Rodian of Tartary. 'I've been on a viking expedition,' he added.

'How old are you?' asked Asmund.

'Twelve,' said Aran.

'There can't be many like you,' said Asmund.

'Back home I had no equal,' said Aran, 'and that's why I made a solemn vow not to return until I'd found someone of my own age and as good as myself. Now, I've heard about a man called Asmund, the son of the king of Halogaland. Could you by any chance tell me anything about him? I've been told that there shouldn't be much between us.'

'I know him very well,' said Asmund. 'He's talking to you.'

'That's a bit of luck,' said Aran. 'And now we'd better try each other out.'

Asmund said he was ready.

They performed every athletic feat known to young men in those days, but were so equally matched there was no choosing between them. Next they wrestled. There was quite a tussle between them, but it was impossible to tell which was the stronger. When they broke off, they were both exhausted.

Then Aran said to Asmund, 'We must never test each other's skill with weapons, since we'd both end up dead. I'd like us to enter a sworn-brotherhood, each of us pledging himself to avenge the other, and sharing equally each other's money, now and in the future.'

It was also a part of their pact that the one who lived the longer should raise a burial mound over the one who was dead, and place in it as much money as he thought fit; and the survivor was to sit in the mound over the dead for three nights, but after that he would be free to go away.

Then they each opened a vein and mixed their blood, which was regarded as an oath. Aran invited Asmund to go with him down to the ships to see what a splendid outfit he had. Since Asmund was staying at that time in Jutland with his grandfather, Earl Ottar, he did as Aran wished.

ARAN'S DEATH

They went down to Aran's fleet, where he had ten longships, all manned with good fighting men. Aran gave Asmund a half-share of his ships and men; Asmund wanted them to sail first to Halogaland to get his own ships and their crews, but Aran insisted on sailing first to his own country and going from there to Halogaland so that people would see they were no common beggars. Asmund said he could have it his own way, and so they put to sea with a fair wind.

Asmund asked whether King Rodian had any other children. Aran said he had another son who was called Herraud. 'His mother's the daughter of the King of Hunland. Herraud's a brave man, very popular, and heir to the throne of Hunland. My father has two brothers, Hrærek and Siggeir, both berserks, very difficult to control, and pretty unpopular among the people. The king puts a lot of trust in them, since they do everything he

56

tells them. They often go plundering and bring back treasures for the king.'

There's nothing more to tell of their voyage until they
reached King Rodian's harbour, where they saw twelve
warships and two dragon-headed longships, so splendid they'd never seen anything like them before. These
ships belonged to two brothers from Ethiopia, called Bull-
Bear and Visin, sons of Earl Gorm. They'd killed King
Rodian, laid much of the country waste and created total
havoc.

When the sworn-brothers heard of this, they had the
alarm sounded, and as soon as the people realized that
Aran had arrived they flocked to him in large numbers.
The marauders rushed down to their ships and a fierce
and deadly battle broke out. For a long time the issue
hung in the balance. Aran jumped aboard Bull-Bear's ship
and laid about him so that everyone on board began to
fall back. Bull-Bear turned to meet him, so Aran struck
a blow at his bald pate, but the sword failed to bite,
particles flew from the skull and the sword broke at
the hilt. Bull-Bear hit back at Aran's shield, splitting it
right through and wounding him badly in the chest. A
broken anchor was lying on the deck. Aran picked it
up and drove it deep into Bull-Bear's head then pushed
him overboard, and Bull-Bear sank down to the sea
bottom.

Visin boarded Asmund's ship and hurled two spears
simultaneously at him. Asmund tried to parry one with
his shield, but it passed right through the shield and into

Asmund's elbow, sticking fast in the bone. But Asmund caught the other spear in flight and hurled it back at Visin straight into his mouth, sinking it up to the middle of the shaft. The spear stuck in the mast as far as the barb, with Visin dangling from it, dead. After that the vikings surrendered, and Asmund had them all killed and thrown overboard. Aran and Asmund went into the town, and the people were very pleased to see Aran. Their wounds were seen to, and afterwards Aran was give the title of king. Then he announced his agreement with Asmund, and gave him a half-share in everything he owned.

Less than a month after their arrival Aran died suddenly one day as he was going into his palace. The corpse was dressed for burial according to custom. Asmund had a burial mound raised over Aran and beside the corpse he put in the mound Aran's horse with a saddle and bridle, his banners and armour, his hawk and hound. Aran was seated on a chair in full armour.

Asmund had another chair brought into the mound and sat himself down there, after which the mound was covered up. During the first night Aran got up from his chair, killed the hawk and hound, and ate them. On the second night he got up again from his chair, killed the horse and tore it to pieces; then he took great bites of horse flesh with his teeth, the blood streaming down from his mouth all the while he was eating. He offered to let Asmund share his meal, but Asmund said nothing. The third night Asmund became very drowsy, and the first thing he knew, Aran had got him by the ears and torn them off. Asmund drew his short-sword and sliced off Aran's head, then he got some fire and burnt Aran to ashes. Asmund went to the rope and was hauled out of the mound, which was then covered up again.

Asmund took all the treasures from the mound with him.

THE BERSERKS

A little later Asmund called the people to a meeting and asked them whether they intended to honour the agreement he had made with Aran. Not many were in favour of the proposal and only the men Aran had given to Asmund were ready to support him.

At this point they happened to look out to sea and saw some ships sailing in. The leaders of this fleet were berserks, the brothers Hrærek and Siggeir. The people ashore weren't too happy about this. Asmund offered to be their leader, but no one was willing to put up a fight, so Asmund went back to his ships with his men.

When the berserks knew what had happened they claimed the whole country for themselves. Asmund told them about his agreement with Aran and said half the country belonged to him. The berserks told him to clear off if he wanted to live. Asmund challenged either of them to a duel, with the kingdom as the stake, but they shouted him down and told their men to get ready for a fight. A fierce battle began. Asmund had a smaller force, and the people didn't dare give him any help, so all his men were killed, and he himself was taken captive. This happened just towards evening.

The berserks decided that Asmund should be executed the following morning on top of Aran's mound and given to Odin as a victory offering, so Asmund was tied to the windlass, but all the others went ashore to see to their wounds and slept in the camp overnight. The brothers were sleeping in a small tent some distance away from the main camp and had only a few men with them.

Now we go back to Asmund, still tied to the windlass. He noticed an iron-lock jutting out from it. This had been given a great blow which had left a rough edge on the iron. Asmund rubbed the rope against this and managed to cut it through as the edge was so sharp. Now that his hands were free he broke the shackles off his feet.

The wind was blowing from the sea, so Asmund cut the anchor line and the ship drifted right up under the forest. In no time he was ashore, and it occurred to him that he might play a bit of a joke on the berserks before making off into the forest, so he made his way to their tent and pulled it down on top of them. Those inside jumped to their feet, but couldn't get out as the tent got in their way. Asmund struck Hrærek on the head, splitting it down to the jaw. Siggeir managed to get out and tried to run into the forest, but Asmund chased after him, and when Siggeir stumbled Asmund struck him from behind, just below the small of his back, slicing it clean through. After that Asmund went into the wood, having already killed ten men as well as the berserks. A search was made for him but he couldn't be found.

Before the day was done Herraud arrived with twenty ships, and everybody was very relieved to see him. He had already heard what had happened, and now he called the people to a meeting where he announced his ownership of the kingdom and asked to be accepted as king. No one spoke against him, so he was made king over the whole country. Those who had supported the berserks were driven away, and Herraud took their property.

Then Asmund went to see King Herraud and greeted him, and the king asked who he was. Asmund told him, and Herraud asked whether he was the man who had killed the berserks. Asmund said he was.

'Why have you come to me then?' asked the king.

'I couldn't think of anything better,' said Asmund, 'and it seemed to me that I'd dropped some pork into your cabbage. I came to see you since I knew very well I couldn't escape. Now I'd like to know what's going to happen to me. I'll defend myself while I can and try to save my life, but I'd accept a better choice if it were offered.'

'I've been told about your agreement with Aran,' said Herraud, 'and it seems a good idea to take you in my brother's place. In my opinion we're well rid of the berserks you killed.'

So Asmund stayed with Herraud, and they got on well together. Asmund asked Herraud to provide him with ships as he wanted to go plundering. Herraud told him to choose his ships and as many men as he liked. He also invited Asmund to come and stay with him whenever he wanted. Asmund picked thirty of Herraud's men and chose one ship. He and Herraud parted the best of friends, each vowing to treat the other as his own brother wherever they might meet again.

From then on Asmund was known as the Berserks-Killer. This is the end of my story, for I am that very man, Asmund.

'I liked that story,' said the old hag. 'How's the gruel getting on, my girl?'

'It's on the boil,' said Skin-Beak.

'It'll be a long while before it's ready,' said the queen. 'And what can you tell us, Egil?'

'Here's how my story begins,' said Egil.

THE GIANT

There was a king called Hring who ruled over the Smalands. He was married to Ingibjorg, daughter of Earl Bjarkmar of Gotaland. They had two children, a son called Egil, and a daughter called Æsa. Egil grew up at his father's court until he was twelve years old. He was quite a handful, troublesome, ambitious, and very hard to control. He used to go around with a crowd of boys and often went with them into the woods to shoot animals and birds.

There was a large lake in the wood, with a number of islands, and Egil and his companions used to go swimming there as they'd grown very skilled at all kinds of sports. One day Egil asked the other boys which of them could swim the farthest into the lake. The outermost island was so far from land that to see it they had to climb the highest trees. So they set out swimming across the lake, thirty of them in all. Everybody agreed that no one should risk going out farther than was safe for him. They went on swimming out into the lake, and some of the sounds between the islands were very wide. Egil was the fastest swimmer and no one could keep up with him. When they had swum a long way from the shore, a mist came down on them so dark that none of them could see the others. Then a cold wind sprang up, and they all lost their bearings. Egil had no idea what had happened to his companions, and wandered about in the water for two days. At last he came to land, now so weak that he had to crawl ashore. He covered himself with moss and lay there overnight, and in the morning he was feeling a bit warmer.

Then a great giant came out of the wood, picked Egil up and tucked him under his arm. 'It's a good thing we've met, Egil,' he said. 'Now I'm offering you a choice: either I kill you on the spot, or else you'll swear an oath to look after my goats as long as I live.'

Finding himself in this predicament, Egil didn't waste much time coming to a decision.

They travelled for many days, and at last came to the cave where the giant had his residence. The giant owned a hundred billy-goats, as well as a good many she-goats. Keeping up their numbers was a matter of life and death to him. Egil started herding the goats but they gave him plenty of trouble. So it went on for some time, but after Egil had been there for a year he ran away. As soon as the giant discovered this, after Egil he went, being so smart that he could trace footprints as readily in water as in snow. Egil had been gone four days before the giant found him in a cave.

The giant said that Egil had treated him worse than he'd deserved. 'So now you're going to get something that'll be the worse for you,' he added.

He took two stones, each of them weighing forty pounds, fastened them with iron clamps to Egil's feet, then told him he could drag this load behind him, and that's what Egil had to put up with for seven years.

The giant was always on his guard, so Egil could see no chance of killing him.

ESCAPE

One day when Egil had gone to look for his goats he came across a cat in the wood. He managed to catch it and brought it home with him. It was late in the evening when he came back, and the fire was smouldering into ashes. The giant asked him why he was so late getting back. Egil answered that he wasn't all that comfortably dressed for walking, and anyway the goats were running all over the place.

'It's a marvel to me,' said the giant, 'how you can find what you're looking for in the dark!'

'That's because of my golden eyes,' said Egil.

'Have you got some other eyes, apart from the ones I've seen?' asked the giant.

'I certainly have,' said Egil.

'Let's have a look at these treasures, then,' said the giant.

'You won't steal them from me?' said Egil.

'They wouldn't be any use to me,' said the giant.

'They're no use to anyone,' said Egil, 'unless I fit them on.'

Then Egil lifted the hem of his cloak and across the fire the giant saw into the cat's eyes, which glittered like two stars.

'There's a treasure worth having,' said the giant. 'Would you sell me these eyes?'

'I'd be the poorer for it,' said Egil. 'But if you'll set me free and take off these shackles, I'll sell them to you.'

'Could you fit them well enough,' asked the giant, 'for me to get the full benefit of them?'

'I'll do my best, said Egil, 'but you'll find the operation a bit painful, as I'll have to lift your eyelids quite a lot to fix the eyes where they ought to be. You'll always have to take them out as soon as it grows light, and only put them in after dark. Now I've got to tie you to this column.'

'You want to kill me,' said the giant, 'that's a dirty trick to play!'

'I'd never do such a thing!' said Egil.

So they made a bargain, and the giant took the shackles off him.

'You've done the right thing,' said Egil, 'and now I'll make you a promise to serve you for the rest of your life.'

Then Egil tied the giant to the column, took a forked rod and drove it into the eyes so that they lay bare on the giant's cheeks. The giant jerked so violently with pain that he snapped the ropes binding him. He fumbled about after Egil and tore the cloak right off him.

'Your luck's run out,' said Egil. 'The gold eyes have fallen into the fire and now they'll be no use to either of us.'

'You've played a dirty trick on me,' said the giant, 'but you'll starve to death in here, and never get out.'

The giant ran to the door and locked it securely, and Egil knew he was in a tricky situation. He had to stay in the cave four nights without food, with the giant on guard all the time.

Then Egil decided what to do. He slaughtered the biggest goat, flayed off the skin, then crept into the skin and sewed it up as tightly as he could.

On the morning of the fourth day Egil drove the goats to the entrance. The giant had placed his thumb against the lintel and his little finger on the doorstep, and the goats had to pass between. Their footsteps echoed on the cave floor.

The giant said, 'It's a sign of stormy weather when the hooves of my goats start to click.'

The goats ran out between his fingers, with Egil bringing up the rear. There wasn't a sound from his hooves.

'You're moving very slowly today, Horny-Beard,' said the giant, 'and you're pretty thick about the shoulders.'

Then he took hold of the goat's wool with both hands, and gave Egil such a shaking that he tore the skin and released him.

'It was lucky for you that I'm blind,' said the giant. 'All the same it's a pity we have to part without your getting some gift from me in recognition of your long service. So take this gold ring.'

It was extremely valuable, and Egil thought it a very fine ring, so he stretched out his hand for it. When the giant felt him take the ring, he pulled Egil towards him and struck at him, cutting off his right ear. Luckily for Egil the giant was blind. Egil cut off the giant's right hand and got the ring.

'I'm going to keep my word,' said Egil, 'and I won't kill you. You'll just have to put up with the pain, and may your last day be your worst.'

With that they parted, and Egil went on his way. For some time he slept out of doors in the wood. When he came out of the wood he saw some viking ships. Their leader was a man called Borgar. Egil joined them and proved himself the bravest of men. They spent the summer plundering, and at Svia Skerries they fought a berserk called Glammad. He had one excellent weapon, a halberd, which could pick out any opponent as soon as the bearer knew his name. Soon after the battle started Glammad jumped aboard Borgar's ship and ran him through with the halberd. Egil was standing near by, his spearhead broken off the shaft. He raised the shaft and drove it hard against Glammad's ear, knocking him overboard. Glammad sank to the bottom with his halberd, and neither ever came up again. Then the vikings stopped fighting and made Egil their leader. He picked out thirty-two men, and went plundering in the Baltic. Plenty happened on his campaign.

THE DWARF

On one occasion Egil lay at anchor in a certain harbour because of bad sailing weather. He went ashore alone and came to a clearing in a wood, where he saw a mound and on it a giant fighting a giantess over a gold ring. She was much weaker than her opponent, who was giving her a hard time. She was wearing a short dress, and her genitalia were very plain to see. She tried to hang on to the ring as best she could. Egil struck at the giant, aiming for the shoulder, but the giant turned quickly so the sword slid down the arm, slicing off a piece of the biceps so big that one man couldn't have lifted it. The giant struck back at Egil and caught him on the arm, cutting it off at the wrist, so that the sword and the hand fell to the ground together. The giant prepared to strike at Egil a second time so Egil had no choice but to run. The giant went after him into the wood, but Egil managed to escape and so they parted. Egil went back to his men with one hand missing and they sailed away.

Egil suffered a lot of pain from the arm. Two days later they came to another harbour and spent a night there. Egil couldn't stand the pain any longer so he got out of bed and took a walk into the forest. He came to a stream and seemed to get some relief by holding the arm in the water and letting it wash over the wound. Then Egil saw a dwarf child coming out of a rock with a pail to fetch water. Egil picked a gold ring off his finger with his teeth and let it slip into the bucket, and the child ran with it back into the rock.

A little later a dwarf came out of the rock and asked who had been so kind to his child. Egil told him his name and added that the way things stood, gold wasn't much use to him.

'I'm sorry to hear that,' said the dwarf. 'Come with me into the rock.' So that's what Egil did.

The dwarf began dressing the stump, and soon the pain had completely gone. In the morning the wound was healed. Then the dwarf set about making him a sword, and from the hilt he made a socket so deep, it reached up to the elbow, where it could be fitted to the arm. So now Egil found it as easy to strike with the sword as if he still had the whole arm. The dwarf gave him a good many more things of value, and they parted the best of friends. Then Egil went back to his men.

'So this,' said Egil, 'is my story up to date, because I'm

the very same man as this Egil whose story I've been telling.'

'You seem to have got yourself into plenty of trouble,' said the queen. 'How is the gruel getting on, my girl?'

'I think it's properly cooked now,' she replied, 'but it's far too hot for anyone to eat while it's like this.'

'I think it'll have cooled by the time I've told my tale, though nothing much has ever happened to me,' said the queen.

QUEEN EAGLE-BEAK'S TALE

There was a giant called Oskrud, who came from Jotunheim. His wife was called Kula, and he had two brothers called Gaut and Hildir. My father Oskrud had eighteen daughters by his wife, and I was the youngest. Everyone agreed I was the best-looking of them all. My father and mother fell ill and died, and then they were put underground and given back to the trolls. We sisters inherited all the money they left, but Gaut and Hilder took the kingdom. They didn't get on with each other.

My father had owned three remarkable treasures: a horn, a chess set, and a gold ring. The brothers took the horn and the chess set, but we sisters managed to hold on to the ring, which was a very valuable thing to have. My sisters used to bully me and I had to wait on them all. Whenever I tried to argue they used to hit me. In the end I felt I couldn't bear it any longer so I made a vow to Thor to give him any goat he wanted if he'd even things up between my sisters and me.

Thor paid us a visit, and went to bed with my eldest sister. He lay with her all night, but my other sisters were so jealous of her that they killed her next morning. Thor did the same to all my sisters, he slept with them all in turn, and they were all killed. But each of them managed to utter a curse on the next, that if she had a child by Thor it would neither grow nor thrive.

Eventually Thor slept with me and gave me this daughter you can see, and the curse has worked well enough on her because she's a yard shorter now than when she was born. Thor gave me everything the sisters left, and he's always been very helpful to me. So I got all the money, but ever since I've been driven by an urge so strong that I don't seem able to live without a man.

One of the men I had to have was Hring, son of the king of the Smalands. I set out to see him, but he'd gone off to Gotaland to ask for the hand of Ingibjorg, the daughter of Earl Bjarkmar. I hurried on my way but when I arrived in Gotaland, Hring was already celebrating his wedding feast and his bride was about to be led into the hall. I lay down in the street intending to play her some dirty trick, but she saw me first and gave me a kick that broke both my thigh-bones. Then she was led into the hall to her seat. I followed her inside, turned myself into a fly, and crept under her clothes with the idea of ripping her belly open at the groin. But she recognized me right away, banged me in the side with a knife handle and broke three of my ribs, so I thought I'd better get out of there.

The day passed, and when the bride was being led to her bed and the bridegroom ushered out of the hall, I picked him up in my arms, and it seemed to me as if I was running down to the sea-cliffs to drown him so no one else would be able to enjoy him. But while I thought I was throwing him off the cliffs, all I did was fling him behind the bed-curtain. He landed on the bed alongside his bride, and I was captured, with no chance of escape. To save my life I was to go to the Underworld and fetch three treasures: a cloak that fire couldn't burn, a drinking horn that could never be emptied, and a chess set that would play by itself whenever anyone challenged it.

THE UNDERWORLD

So I went down to the Underworld and saw King Snow, and for sixty goats and a pound of gold I bought the horn from him. A poison-cup the size of twelve casks had been prepared for his queen, and I had to drink this on her behalf as well. Ever since then I've always been a bit troubled with heartburn.

From there I went to Mount Lucanus where I found three women (if you could call them women, for I looked like a baby compared with them), in charge of the chess set. I managed to get half of the chess set off them, but when they found it missing and realized it was me, they asked me to give it back. I refused and challenged any one of them to take it away from me, staking the chess set against all the gold I could carry. They thought this wouldn't be too hard for them, and so one of them made for me, grabbed hold of my hair and tore half of it off along with my left ear and the whole of my cheek. She was hard on me, but I didn't give in, I put my fingers into her eyes and gouged them out. Then I tried to throw her, but she caught her foot in a rock crevice so I dislocated her hip joint. With that we parted.

Then the second sister rushed at me and gave me a punch on the nose, so that she broke it. It's been regarded as rather a blemish on my looks ever since, and I lost three teeth as well. I got hold of her breasts and tore them both off down to the ribs and then the flesh of her belly and the entrails too.

Next the third sister attacked me, the smallest of them. I meant to gouge her eyes out just as I'd done to the other, but she bit off two of my fingers. I put her down with a heel-throw, and she fell flat on her back. She begged for mercy, and I told her that I'd only spare her life if she gave me the whole chess set. She didn't waste any time over that. Then I told her to get up, and as a parting gift she gave me a magic glass. If a man looks into it, I can give him the shape of anyone I choose. If I want I can blind whoever looks into it.

Next I went to the Underworld to fetch the cloak, and there I met the Prince of Darkness. As soon as he saw me said he wanted to sleep with me. I guessed he must be

Odin because he only had one eye. He told me I could have the cloak if I was willing to fetch it from where it was kept. I had to jump across a huge fire to get it. First I slept with Odin, then I jumped over the fire and got the cloak, but ever since I've had no skin to my body.

After doing all this I went back home to Hring and Ingibjorg and gave them the treasurers, but before we parted I had to swear an oath never to avenge myself on them. So, not feeling too happy about the affair, I came back to my own home. I'll remember that girl in Gotaland as long as I live. Later I'll tell you about the little games I've had to play with my brothers. How's the gruel getting on, girl?

'I think it's just about cool enough,' she said.

'Serve it up then,' said the hag.

After they had finished their meal the foster-brothers were shown to their bed, and slept through the night.

RECOVERY

In the morning the brothers woke up early. The old hag joined them, and when they asked her what time it was, she told them that they could stay there all day. So they got up and dressed. The old hag was very hospitable. They sat down to a meal, and now she offered them good ale and fine cooking, and inquired where they were going and what business they had. They told her all about their business and asked her whether she could give them any idea of what had happened to King Hertrygg's daughters.

'I don't know how successful you'll be in your search for them,' she said. 'But first of all, I'd better tell you what happened after the death of the giant Oskrud. The brothers didn't agree about which of them should be king, they both felt they had the right. Anyway, they did agree that the one who could get the more nobly born and talented princess should be king. Gaut was the first to go and he carried off King Hertrygg's elder daughter Hild; then Hildir went and carried off Bekkhild. Both girls are here now in Jotunheim, but I don't think they'll be easy to get free. They're to be married at Christmas, and all the giants will be gathered to decide which of the sisters has the greater skill.'

'Things are looking up,' said Asmund, 'now we know where the sisters are. It would make all the difference if you'd help us.'

'The only reason why I keep up my family ties with Gaut and Hildir,' she said, 'is so that I shouldn't be under any obligation to them. It's due more to my own good faith than to anything on their part. You'd better take a rest here for today, and I'll show you my treasures.'

This suited them very well. When the table had been cleared, the old hag led them into a large side-chamber off the main cave. Inside stood a number of boxes which she unlocked, full of a great many rare and precious things, which they very much enjoyed looking at. Finally, the old hag picked up a small casket and opened it. A sweet fragrance came from it and, inside, Egil recognized his hand with his gold ring on the finger. It seemed to him as if the hand was still warm and steaming, and the veins throbbing.

'Do you know anything about this hand, Egil?' asked the old hag.

'I certainly do,' said Egil, 'and I recognize this gold ring my mother once gave me. But how did you come by my hand?'

'I can tell you about that,' said the old hag. 'My brother Gaut came and asked me to sell him my precious gold ring, but I wouldn't part with it. Some time later when my daughter was out tending the goats, he went to her and gave her a certain drink, which started her screaming and she couldn't be stopped until I brought the ring to her where she was lying on top of a mound. When I arrived with the ring Gaut appeared and wanted to take it away from me. I stood up to him, and there was quite a tussle between us. I was just about to loosen my hold on the ring when a stranger came out of the wood – very much like you, Egil. He took a great swing at the giant but the giant cut off his hand, and after that both of them ran off into the wood. I picked up the hand and ever since then I've looked after it and kept it wrapped in life-herbs so that it wouldn't die. I think we agree, Egil, that this man must have been you. If you'll risk letting me reopen the wound, I'll try to graft the hand on to the arm.'

'I don't see any risk in that,' said Egil. She took the socket off his arm and deadened the arm so that Egil didn't feel any pain when she trimmed the stump. Then she put life-herbs on it, wrapped it in silk and held it firmly for the rest of the day. Egil could feel the life flow in. The old hag put him to bed and told him to stay there until his hand was healed. It was fully healed in three days, and now he found the hand no stiffer than it had been when the arm was still whole, though it appeared to have a red thread around it.

They asked the old hag what she would advise them to do, and she told them to stay there till the wedding.

'My partner, Skrogg, lives not far from here and if we manage to outwit my brothers, I'd like Skrogg and myself to profit from it.' So time passed till Christmas.

THE WEDDING

Now we take up the story at the point where the brothers Gaut and Hildir called the giants together to a meeting, to which they came from all over Jotunheim. Skrogg, as the giants' lawman, was there as well. The two princesses were led before the gathering with the masterpieces they had created. Brynhild had made a carpet with this remarkable property, that you could fly on it through the air and land wherever you wanted. You could even carry a heavy load on it. Bekkhild had made a shirt that no weapon could bite, nor would anyone wearing it ever grow tired when swimming.

Now an argument started about which of the sisters had shown the greater skill. The final decision was a matter for all the giants, but they couldn't reach an agreement, so Skrogg was asked to make the award. His verdict was that Brynhild was the more beautiful of the two, and that her carpet was made with the greatest skill, 'and so Gaut shall be the king and marry Brynhild, but each brother rule over half the kingdom'.

After that the assembly broke up.

The brothers invited the leaders and all the most important people to the double wedding.

Skrogg came back home and told the old hag what had happened at the assembly and when the wedding was to be. They talked things over for some time and she told him that she wanted to help the brothers. She asked him to come with a large following and whatever else they needed. Skrogg said he would do as she wanted.

When the time had come for the wedding the old hag, and the foster-brothers with her, got ready to go. One of them was to be called Fjalar and the other Frosti. She made them look into the mirror, and then they seemed the size of giants, though much better-looking. She provided them with the right sort of clothes, and so they travelled on till they came to the brothers' residence called Gjallandi Bridge. The giants were drinking; and when the old hag walked into the cave, each glanced at the other. She went up to Gaut and gave him a polite greeting.

He made a proper acknowledgement. 'This is something that's never happened before, your paying us a visit,' he said.

'Things aren't quite as they should be,' she answered.

'Relations have been pretty cool between us till now, and I won't deny that I'm to blame for that. I realize now, my dear Gaut, that you've good luck on your side: you've found an excellent wife, and as my contribution I'd like to offer something we've quarrelled over in the past. I'm going to give you that fine ring, a perfect bed-gift for your wife, and my friendship with it. We owe it to our family ties to be generous to each other.'

Gaut said he was truly grateful '– and, by the way, where did you find these good-looking men?'

She told him they were the sons of King Dumb of the Dumb Sea, 'and you won't easily find anyone in Jotunheim to equal them, particularly in matters of etiquette. I'd meant them to be in attendance at your wedding.'

Then she handed the ring over to Gaut who thanked her for it. She was to serve at the wedding, everything was to be done exactly as Fjalar and Frosti wanted, and they were given keys to all the money boxes.

The guests were now beginning to arrive and soon there was a large gathering. The old hag was in charge, and everything had to be done according to her instructions. Skrogg the Lawman was the most respected of all the honoured guests.

The old hag explained in a whisper to the sisters who her companions were. 'So you can cheer up, now,' she added.

This made them very happy, for they hadn't felt particularly enthusiastic about their wedding, but the giants were delighted to see them in a cheerful mood and thanked their kinswoman for her good services. When all the guests had been settled and the brothers had sat down, the brides were led inside. The giants were making boorish jokes in loud voices. Skrogg the Lawman was sitting on one side with the farmers, and Gaut and Hildir on the opposite bench with their own followers. Eagle-Beak was sitting next to the brides, and helped by some other huge ladies she gave them advice about how they should conduct themselves. Fjalar and Frosti served the ladies and there was no shortage of strong drink.

So as the evening wore on, the guests were becoming quite drunk. Then Eagle-Beak got to her feet and called the lawman and the foster-brothers over to her, telling them to bring in the wedding presents. The magic carpet, the shirt, the fine chess set that belonged to the brothers, the fine ring that had belonged to Eagle-Beak, and many other things of value were carried into the cave. Skrogg the Lawman handed over the wedding presents, and the old hag took them into her charge. She spread the carpet on the ground, put the other treasures on top, and told her daughter Skin-Beak to fetch the gold and silver.

Eagle-Beak went back into the cave and asked Frosti to come with her. They went to the place where Gaut and Brynhild were meant to sleep. She told Frosti that behind the bedpost he'd find Gaut's famous sword, the only weapon that could wound him. She also said that Fjalar and Hildir would be meeting again in another place, and warned the foster-brothers to be ready for a test of their manhood.

After that Eagle-Beak went back to the main cave and called out that it was bedtime for the brides. Fjalar and Frosti took the brides by the hand and settled them down on the carpet. Then the old hag made the carpet take off. She gave her daughter the mirror and told her to go to the entrance of the cave and hold the mirror to the face of all those who came out. The sisters soared in the air on the carpet, along with everything that was on it.

Now a lively dance started up in the cave as the bridegrooms were about to be led outside.

CASUALTIES

The cave had three doors. Skrogg the Lawman with his party was in charge of one of them and Skin-Beak was in charge of the door through which the common people went. The bridegrooms were led through the third door and just outside it were two smaller caves on either side, hung with fine tapestries, where they were to sleep.

When the two giants had passed through the door, each of them went into his own room. Egil accompanied Hildir into one, walking ahead. As Hildir entered the cave Egil turned on him, got hold of his hair and swung his shortsword, aiming at the throat, but Hildir struck back at him quickly, so Egil was knocked against the rock face, and the skin of his forehead broken. It was quite a wound and bled freely, but the short-sword caught the giant's nose and sliced it off. The severed piece was big enough to make a full load for a horse. Hildir managed to get outside and shouted that he had been tricked. The giants inside heard this and made a rush for the exit, but didn't find it easy to get by. At one door Skrogg the Lawman killed all who tried to get out and at the other Skin-Beak blinded everyone with the mirror. So the giants ran to and fro inside the cave, not knowing which way to turn and roaring and banging about.

Gaut heard this and realized what must have happened. When he came to his private cave he saw that the bride was missing, so he rushed over to the bed intending to grab his sword, but found it missing too. Asmund raised the sword and aimed at Gaut, though he didn't take account of the low ceiling, so the sword caught the rock and bit through it. But the point of the sword caught Gaut's eyebrow, cut down through the eye, the cheekbone and collarbone, and sliced clean through the breast to sever the ribs. Gaut managed to get outside where he picked up a huge boulder and hurled it at Asmund, hitting him in the chest and knocking him flat. Gaut made an effort to rush towards him but his entrails got tangled up with his feet and he dropped down dead.

Asmund stood up and began looking around for Egil. At last he came to where Egil and Hildir were fighting it out. Blood was pouring out of Egil's eye from the wound he'd received, and his strength was obviously failing. Asmund caught hold of both Hildir's feet, Egil held on to his head and between them they broke his neck. That was the end of him.

Asmund and Egil went back to Skrogg the Lawman. He'd killed ninety giants, and the rest of them were begging for mercy. The giants who went out through the door guarded by Skin-Beak walked straight over the cliff and killed themselves.

The foster-brothers spent the night in the cave and Eagle-Beak joined them there. In the morning they got hold of all the valuables in the cave and went back home with the old hag. The sisters had already arrived and were delighted to see them. They all stayed there over winter and enjoyed the finest hospitality.

In the spring they got ready to set out and rejoin their own men, but before parting they gave Jotunheim to Eagle-Beak and Skrogg the Lawman. Everyone parted the best of friends. The foster-brothers took away with them all the treasures mentioned above. They came to their own men in the last week of winter and there was a happy reunion between them.

As soon as the wind was favourable they put to sea and kept going until they got back to King Hertrygg.

ANOTHER WEDDING

King Hertrygg gave them and his daughters a great welcome. They brought him a good many treasures and told him exactly what had happened to them on the trip. The king thanked them handsomely for the journey they had made.

A little later the king called the people to a meeting, and reminded them of the promise he had made to the man who found his daughters. The king asked the foster-brothers whether they'd prefer to get their reward in gold and silver, but both gave the same reply, that they'd rather have his daughters as long as the girls were willing to marry them. The girls knew that the foster-brothers had saved their lives and said they wouldn't want any other men for husbands if they could marry these. So the outcome was that Egil married Bekkhild and Asmund married Brynhild.

The king had preparations made for a wedding feast. Egil said he wanted first to go back home to see if his father was still alive and what his hopes might be concerning the throne, which he thought he had a right to. Asmund said he wanted to go east to Tartary to invite his foster-brother Herraud to the wedding. The time for the wedding was fixed and also the time for their return. There's nothing to say about their travels except that they went well.

When Egil arrived in Gotaland, he went to see his father who completely failed to recognize him, as he thought he must have died long before. He told his father in detail what had happened to him (as we've already described it here) and showed the scar on his wrist where his hand had been cut off. He showed him too the socketed sword the dwarf had made him. They asked the dwarf Regin to fix a handle on it, and after that it was a fine weapon. Egil invited his father, mother and sister to the wedding and when they came to King Hertrygg, Herraud and Asmund had already arrived.

The king gave them all a splendid welcome and it wasn't very long before a great feast was in full swing. There were many different kinds of musical instrument to be heard there and many distinguished people to be seen. No expense had been spared to get the best of everything available in that part of the world.

During the feast Egil and Asmund entertained the guests with stories about their travels, and it's said that to prove the truth of their tale, both Skin-Beak and Eagle-Beak were there and vouched for their story. Queen Ingibjorg recognized Eagle-Beak, and they were fully reconciled.

The feast lasted a whole month, and when it was over all the guests went back home with splendid gifts. Egil gave Herraud the shirt that Bekkhild had made and Asmund gave him the ring that had belonged to the old hag and the sword as well, that had belonged to Gaut.

King Hertrygg was getting on in years, so he asked Egil to stay with him. He said he didn't expect to live much longer. Egil said he wanted first to go home to Gotaland but that he would be back within twelve months, and the king gave his permission. Asmund invited Herraud to come with him to Halogaland and Herraud agreed to go.

Eagle-Beak went back home to Jotunheim: Queen Ingibjorg gave her a butter-keg so big she could only just lift it and said they would think it a rare thing in Jotunheim. Asmund gave her two flanks of bacon so heavy they weighed a ton. The old hag appreciated these gifts more than if she'd been given a load of gold, and they all parted the best of friends.

THE END OF THE STORY

Asmund and Herraud embarked, and sailed off in the fine dragon-headed longship that had belonged to Visin and Bull-Bear. There's nothing to tell of their voyage until they arrived north in Halogaland. When the people there saw their dragon ship King Ottar remarked on how far these men must have come.

As soon as they landed, they pitched their tents ashore. Asmund went with eleven men to see his father and greeted him respectfully. The king failed to recognize him, but his mother knew him at once and put her arms round him. The king asked who was this stranger his wife was being so friendly to and Asmund gave him the answer. Soon an excellent feast was under way, and they spent a month there enjoying the best of hospitality. They told the king all about their travels and he thought they'd had plenty of success and good luck.

Herraud told Asmund that he wanted them to go east together to Gotaland to ask for the hand of Æsa, Hring's daughter. Asmund thought this a good idea, and as soon as the wind was favourable they sailed east to Gotaland.

86

Egil and Hring gave them a great welcome. Herraud spoke up and asked for Æsa's hand. This was well received and she was given to him with a large dowry. The wedding was celebrated at once and the feast went very well.

After the feast Egil and Herraud sailed to the Baltic, but Asmund stayed behind as he was to be king of Gotaland should Hring die. By the time they got back to Tartary King Hertrygg was dead, so Egil was made king, and he and Bekkhild lived there from then on. Herraud took over his own kingdom a little later. Neither of them came north to Scandinavia after that.

Asmund went back home to Halogaland and ruled there for many years. His son Armod married Edny, daughter of King Hakon Hamundarson of Denmark, and a great progeny has come down from them. This Armod was killed in his bath by Starkad the Old, and that was Starkad's last crime.

Brynhild didn't live long, so Asmund married again. His second wife was the daughter of Sultan, the king of the Saracens. Asmund was supposed to come to the wedding in a single ship, as they intended to trick him, but Asmund had a ship built that he called the *Gnod*, the biggest ship known to have been built north of the Ægean Sea. Because of this ship he was nicknamed Gnod-Asmund, and he is considered the greatest of all the ancient kings who did not rule over the major kingdoms.

Asmund was killed near Læso Island and over three thousand men with him. It's said that Odin ran him through with a spear and that Asmund jumped over-board, but the *Gnod* sank to the bottom with its cargo and nothing of the ship or the cargo has ever been found.

And so we end this story.

READ MORE IN PENGUIN

For complete information about books available from Penguin and how to order them, please write to us at the appropriate address below. Please note that for copyright reasons the selection of books varies from country to country.

IN THE UNITED KINGDOM: Please write to *Dept. EP, Penguin Books Ltd, Bath Road, Harmondsworth, Middlesex UB7 ODA*.

IN THE UNITED STATES: Please write to *Consumer Sales, Penguin USA, P.O. Box 999, Dept. 17109, Bergenfield, New Jersey 07621-0120*. VISA and MasterCard holders call 1-800-253-6476 to order Penguin titles.

IN CANADA: Please write to *Penguin Books Canada Ltd, 10 Alcorn Avenue, Suite 300, Toronto, Ontario M4V 3B2*.

IN AUSTRALIA: Please write to *Penguin Books Australia Ltd, P.O. Box 257, Ringwood, Victoria 3134*.

IN NEW ZEALAND: Please write to *Penguin Books (NZ) Ltd, Private Bag 102902, North Shore Mail Centre, Auckland 10*.

IN INDIA: Please write to *Penguin Books India Pvt Ltd, 706 Eros Apartments, 56 Nehru Place, New Delhi 110 019*.

IN THE NETHERLANDS: Please write to *Penguin Books Netherlands bv, Postbus 3507, NL-1001 AH Amsterdam*.

IN GERMANY: Please write to *Penguin Books Deutschland GmbH, Metzlerstrasse 26, 60594 Frankfurt am Main*.

IN SPAIN: Please write to *Penguin Books S. A., Bravo Murillo 19, 1° B, 28015 Madrid*.

IN ITALY: Please write to *Penguin Italia s.r.l., Via Felice Casati 20, I-20124 Milano*.

IN FRANCE: Please write to *Penguin France S. A., 17 rue Lejeune, F-31000 Toulouse*.

IN JAPAN: Please write to *Penguin Books Japan, Ishikiribashi Building, 2-5-4, Suido, Bunkyo-ku, Tokyo 112*.

IN GREECE: Please write to *Penguin Hellas Ltd, Dimocritou 3, GR-106 71 Athens*.

IN SOUTH AFRICA: Please write to *Longman Penguin Southern Africa (Pty) Ltd, Private Bag X08, Bertsham 2013*.